GHOSTSHOW LIVE!

CHRISTOPHER DEGNI

To my parents Sandra and Vito Degni, who always told
me I could be whatever I wanted to be

Chapter One

Tessie Gold stood stuck in place in her too-small living room, holding the next round of her mother's meds arranged carefully on a plate.

"I don't need your help," said the old woman, voice thick with stubbornness and bile.

"Take the pills, Ma."

The house barely fit Tessie, and the addition of her mother had increased her feeling of claustrophobia. No matter how diligently she cleaned, a hint of stale urine tainted the living room; the air was warm and disconcertingly moist, almost smothering, thanks to the ancient humidifier in the corner vomiting its acrid steam. Tessie's last refuge was a small room at the rear of the house: her den. Her mother's voice reached everywhere, though.

It was only a matter of time before Tessie would be forced to call hospice—if she could swing it. Her residual checks were dwindling. Her sister Natalie had yet to offer any monetary support or comfort of any kind. *I gave that up a long time ago*, she'd told Tessie. *Yeah, I remember*, Tessie had replied. Meanwhile, her mother's house had been liquidated and poured into medical bills. If it weren't for the government assistance, her mother would be on the street, dragging Tessie along with her. Natalie didn't seem to care.

But Tessie couldn't let her mother die alone, no matter how much the woman deserved it.

Tessie proffered the assortment of pills, but her mother pushed them away. "No more!"

"Ma, you have to take them."

"Take them nothing." Her mother's hand shot out; Tessie flinched, an old habit unbroken, then absent-mindedly rubbed the scar on her cheekbone, a hated reminder of childhood days. Her mother had knocked the plate out of her hand, scattering the caplets across the floor. For a dying woman, she was quick when she wanted to be. Her face was thinner than Tessie had ever remembered, her eyes sunken and hair stringy. But she was rancorous as ever. Each day, a bit more of her physical self disappeared, even as the specter of her at full strength lingered. Tessie entertained the thought of her evaporating completely before her body gave out. If only it were that tidy.

"Dammit, Ma!" Tessie knelt to find the pills—the long purplish one, and the two small round white ones (each labeled with a different set of letters and numbers in the world's tiniest font), the yellow-and-red caplet, the one blue and speckled like a robin's egg, and a pair of translucent golden ovoids. Tessie remembered seven, always seven: seven in the morning, seven at noon, and seven at night. Every morning, noon, and night. And a battle every time.

Across the room, the tarnished bronze mail slot squeaked open, and a thick yellow envelope shot through. It thudded against the ground, followed by the swish of a half-dozen smaller envelopes, several banded in bright red. A rush of cold air swooshed along the ground, its tendrils finding Tessie a scant moment after the package landed. Tessie involuntarily shook out a chill. At least the breeze offered fleeting relief from the stifling humidity.

"That could be..." mumbled Tessie to herself.

"I don't know why you're bothering."

"Maybe the same reason I'm bothering with you," said Tessie, guilt grabbing her before she'd even finished the sentence.

"Then let me die," said her mother. "I didn't ask for your help. I don't need it."

Tessie sighed. She gathered the pills, returned them to the plate, and headed to the kitchen. She'd try again in an hour or two, when her mother was feeling less ornery.

Curiosity about the envelope tugged at her. Tessie returned to the living room, and the lingering cold air struck her like a wall. It should have warmed up by now.

"I'm freezing," said her mother. "Turn up the heat." She coughed, showing her displeasure.

"It's a draft," replied Tessie.

"There's no draft," said her mother. Another fake cough.

Her mother was right. Tessie crossed to the door and felt for air currents, but found nothing. She picked up the pale yellow package, and the old woman broke into a violent coughing fit, for real this time. Tessie was helpless to do anything but let the spasms take their course. Her mother's face contorted, and her eyes rolled back and showed nothing but whites. A mischievous half-smile flickered across her face and disappeared, and then her coughing subsided and her breathing returned to normal.

Tessie's shoulders relaxed. It would be such a relief when the old woman was gone.

The envelope radiated cold. Maybe the air outside was more bitter than she'd thought. She placed her hand on the door, expecting to feel the penetrating chill, but the metal felt warm.

"You're too old to go back to school," wheezed her mother. "You shouldn't have gone the first time." She began coughing again.

"Save your breath, Ma," said Tessie. "And drink some water. You're going to hack up a lung."

"You're still broke from the first time around."

"We're not discussing this."

"You don't have the money," said her mother. "Or the brains."

Tessie turned away from her mother and contemplated the envelope. She'd already received rejection after rejection. One application left: the University of Maine. She'd been expecting a decision by email, but sometimes admission packages preceded the formal offer letter, and as everyone knew, rejections were thin and acceptances thick, like the envelope she now held. The back of the large envelope faced her, blank, and she hoped for nothing more than to see the pine tree seal of the university on the obverse side. She closed her eyes and flipped it over.

When she opened her eyes, she was met not with formal letterhead, but a scrawl of vaguely familiar handwriting. The top left corner of the envelope held an unfamiliar return address and a cartoonish sketch of a ghost.

It couldn't be.

"What is it?" asked her mother threateningly.

"It's from Rob."

"That dirt bag?" Her mother scowled and spat on the floor next to her bed.

"Jesus, Ma, what the hell?"

"Tricking you into becoming an actress. Waitressing was good enough for me—"

"He didn't trick me into anything," said Tessie. "And waitressing wasn't good enough for me."

"Uppity," sneered her mother.

She'd last heard from her friend Rob four years prior, when the reality show they hosted wrapped. They hadn't seen each other since.

Tessie ran her fingers under the flap of the envelope, ripped it open, and pulled out a sheet of paper folded in half.

Tess, Found a cool new house! See what you think. We have an opportunity to film a show: a LIVE show! Can you imagine? Call me for details. –Rob

Tessie felt a sharp pain on her finger as she returned the sheet to the envelope. The paper cut didn't bleed at first, but it exposed a sliver of delicate pink skin. She sucked the wound, but it made her finger sting more.

"It's a sign," said her mother, watching the whole display.

Tessie glared as she retreated to her den, away from the old woman's prying eyes, and tossed the envelope onto her desk to consider later that night.

··········

Rob's "cool new house" sneered at Tessie and she felt waves of animus rising like heat from the photograph, bringing the blood to her cheeks and curdling the contents of her stomach. A drop of sweat crashed from her forehead onto the image, distorting the window in the upper right gable and ruining one of the house's eyes, increasing its malevolence. She closed the manila folder, like slamming the door on an unwanted guest, and felt back to normal.

No way, she thought, *I'm out.*

Tessie hadn't been able to warm up since the envelope had been delivered. Even now her clammy skin rose in goosebumps. She rubbed her arms. Muffled snores emanated from the front room of the house like bursts of static on the radio, her mother sleeping not-so-soundly.

She examined the awards on her wall for the first time in years: four nearly-identical plaques, each adorned with a bas-relief specter that reminded her of Munch's *Scream* (no one said trophy designers were original) and an inscribed rectangular panel. The engravings differed only in date.

BEST TELEVISUAL ACHIEVEMENT—HORROR/REALITY
"GHOSTSHOW WITH SILVER AND GOLD"
TESSIE GOLD AND ROB SILVER

20—

Below them hung a tattered *Discover* magazine cover, framed to preserve its remaining integrity, the vibrant blue sea of the original faded to a mottled consistency that more resembled a hazy sky. She'd spent long hours in her youth staring at that cover, imagining a better life somewhere away, somewhere her mother couldn't reach her.

The nausea returned as Tessie considered reopening the folder and reading through the dossier in its entirety. The thought of crawling back to reality TV was almost too much for her stomach to bear. Pretending to unearth lost spectral secrets. Playing the dunce when they found "evidence." The hate mail—she *still* received letters from time to time—calling her all manner of "stupid bitch," each one more colorful and invective-filled than the last.

But a new show would come with money. Maybe enough to stanch the bleeding. Let her mother die with dignity and take the weight off her own chest. Tessie wished she'd had an agent of her own, but who would take her, being out of the game so long? Rob had negotiated the deals for the both of them, and he'd always been good to her.

It was Rob who plucked her from obscurity when she was waitressing for less than minimum wage and performing in low-budget commercials for the local car dealership; ads that ran during sports radio simulcasts and at three in the morning, when the sick and disturbed watched. Maybe that's how he'd found her. Maybe he had a bit of the sickness in him.

She'd practiced her audition before they met, but they hit it off so thoroughly she didn't have to resort to her prepared material. She'd had worse coworkers—and certainly worse jobs.

Besides, it was one show, one house, no more than a long weekend. Not exactly a resort getaway, but a mini-vacation nonetheless. She didn't believe the supernatural stuff anyway, no matter what "televisual achievements" they'd produced. She was the resident skeptic, Rob the believer. It's why they worked so well together.

Forty-eight houses over their run, and not one shred of evidence of the supernatural. Rob held a different opinion, partially thanks to Tessie's covert behind-the-scenes work. He enjoyed the mystery of the unknown so much, though, that the deception felt harmless. It created compelling television, kicked Rob's career into high gear, and paid for Tessie's college degree.

They'd called it quits by mutual understanding, although Tessie would have pushed for a wrap had Rob not agreed. She'd thought little about Rob until that afternoon, when the dossier arrived in the mail. Now the shadow of reality TV had returned.

"What's so special about this one?" she whispered as she reopened the folder.

Tessie felt none of the anxiety that had accosted her previously. The photograph depicted the same house, smeared eye and all. The vestiges of a sneer remained. Underneath the first photograph were several more: pictures taken at different times of day and year, and from different angles, and always the same trace of a smirk. The dossier also contained several photos of a different house (this one was a garrison, not a craftsman, but shared the same condescending facial expression somehow); a detail about the pictures caught Tessie's interest, but she couldn't identify what. Lining them up, she flipped her eyes back and forth, like trying to solve a spot-the-differences puzzle. The trees were the same. Taller—older—in the photos of the original house, but it was unmistakable: knots, crooks, and branches all in the same places. The garrison must have been demolished, replaced by the craftsman.

The dossier contained a short note about the "Hardie House," as it was known locally, named after the family that had razed and rebuilt the structure and still ended up fleeing in fear. It confirmed Tessie's suspicions: first, the house had been remade, and second, Rob's interest stemmed from the persistence of bad fortune across the two incarnations. Tessie had to admit they'd never seen such a situation and it could make for a unique show. She glanced at the clock—one after midnight—hesitated, then punched Rob's number on her cell.

Rob picked up before the first ring finished.

"Tessie! The package arrived, I presume?" She'd been right—he sounded wide awake, though the phone connection made it hard to tell. Static fizzled on the other end of the line.

"*This* is the best you've got?" she asked. "After all these years?" Her voice echoed back at her, *th--e yea--*, faded, clipped, and overlapping her own speech, throwing her timing off.

"Oh, c'mon Tessie! Multiple families, multiple houses, multiple incidents. We couldn't ask for more. It's even better: we checked the archives, and there's no record of it being an ancient graveyard or anything hackneyed like that. It has to be the house."

"The house's spirit jumped?" she asked. Rob's enthusiasm made Tessie smile. She recalled their easy rapport on set: him playing up his excited goofball ghostbuster personality, and her reacting with good-natured sarcastic skepticism, the lens magnifying their personalities. "That's a new one. Strong narrative hook. Where'd you dig this house up anyway?" she asked. *Hou-- up any-ay* returned to her ear, distorted and a register too low.

The line hissed and popped in the space between words, and unfamiliar voices whispered snakelike syllables in unfamiliar languages. *Damn crossed signals.*

"Screw that, strong narrative hook!" said Rob. "It's demonic, and we're going to prove it!"

In a burst of clarity, one of the voices spat *fucking demon*—or maybe Tessie simply misheard a warped echo of Rob's words.

"Rob," said Tessie, thinking about blowing his mind with the truth, "I should tell you..." No, there was no need. "I'm not sure. It's been over four years. We've been off longer than we were on. I hadn't considered returning."

"Well, consider it now, Tessie. I don't want to do this without you."

The shadow conversation turned to sibilant laughter, a blunted shrieking which threatened to take over the connection.

"I'm sorry, Rob, I can't do it," she said, pausing, then blurting, "unless the money is good." She amended herself, quickly adding, "Not that I'd do it only for the money. I'd love to work with you again, I really would, but my mother's sick, and there's too much to do, and I have so much on my—"

"Tessie," interrupted Rob, "I'm not going to force you. But the payday's good, if that's what it'll take. And sounds like you could use the time away."

Tessie's spirit lifted with the thought of a long weekend far from the old woman's torments. "I don't know..." *To--ents*, echoed Tessie's voice. Had she said that out loud?

"It'll be like old times," continued Rob. She could tell by his wry tone he knew he had her on the ropes. "I'll send you the contract. I have a good feeling about this."

"That makes one of us."

"Aren't we a regular Mulder and Scully?" said Rob. "Which one are you? I've never actually seen that show."

"I'd be Scully. And she was only wrong because the story demanded it."

"No one watches a show where Scully's right," he replied. Tessie could hear the smug smile in his voice. "So are you going to join me?"

Tessie took a deep breath. She felt Rob's anticipation. One last show for old times' sake. "I'm in."

Long after the call ended, the connection's hissing and popping and shrieking haunted Tessie until she fell into a merciful slumber, dreamless and deep into the jaws of the night.

Chapter Two

Natalie's house, small and neat, smiled at Tessie from behind its picket fence, the once lush green lawn fading into patches of brown brought on by the fall. Freshly painted shingles. Gleaming windows. It represented everything Tessie was not.

What was she even doing here? She never should have agreed to join Rob. She had no right to decide before arranging care for her mother. She couldn't leave the woman and she couldn't afford an in-home nurse, even assuming the money came through. One option remained. Now she felt like a beggar, asking for a favor she didn't deserve, and the sign in the corner of the window said "No soliciting."

She'd never seen Natalie's house. They traded anodyne greetings once a year around the holidays, though even those had grown less frequent. Natalie, with her talk of independence, had made it all of twenty minutes away. Maybe twenty minutes was enough. She could've lived in another country for as much as Tessie saw her.

Tessie conjured an image of her sister as she knew her in childhood—an accomplice, a protector, a friend—and marched to the front door. She pursed her lips and raised a fist to knock. She paused for several moments, and quickly as her resolve came, it left her. As she headed back to her car, she heard a soft voice, strange and familiar at once, say, "Heya sis."

Natalie stood holding the door open, her face drawn and melancholy, with a look of mild impatience, like she'd been expecting Tessie to visit and Tessie was late to the party. "Come on in. I'll put on some tea."

The house's interior was as meticulously cared for as its exterior. Spotless hardwood floors, shined to a mirror. Not much on the walls, but what was there was expensive and tasteful. Her sister was now the kind to hang original artwork?

"Sit," said Natalie, and Tessie sunk herself into a marshmallow couch. Natalie disappeared to the kitchen. The house smelled of chamomile and bergamot. And baby powder.

The end table held a framed wedding picture, but her sister was single. Tessie picked up the photograph for a better look. Natalie stood in the sand, barefoot and wearing an elegant linen sundress and an understated smile, her groom at her side, the backdrop a dark blue sky streaked with angry thunderclouds. Natalie's hair and dress fluttered in the wind along with the swaying palm trees.

"You're married?" said Tessie accusingly at her sister when she re-entered the room, bearing a tray with two teacups.

Natalie looked at her with mournful eyes, saying nothing in return.

"You eloped," declared Tessie. She replaced the photo on the end table and noticed a small, pastel yellow walkie-talkie.

"And a baby? I have a…"

"Niece," said Natalie softly, placing the tea ensemble onto the low table in the center of the room.

"Why didn't you tell me?"

Natalie's eyes became glassy. She trembled as she held back tears. "You didn't ask."

"But…" Tessie struggled to think of the last time she and her sister had talked. Every Christmas, like clockwork, except they'd missed the last one nearly a year ago, and maybe the one or two before that.

Natalie pulled herself together. "Why are you here?"

"Can I meet her?" asked Tessie. "What's her name?"

"Anastasia. She's napping now. Maybe when she wakes up." Natalie's eyes had hardened.

Tessie paced across the living room. She formed the words of her request in her mind. Her sister, married with a child—this would complicate things. She'd not want to see their mother even more so now.

"I need a favor." Tessie's cheeks burned as she put herself into such a vulnerable position. Natalie nodded at her.

"I need you..." Tessie continued, "I need you to watch Ma for a few days."

Natalie was a statue. "I have no mother," she finally said.

"You do," said Tessie, "and she's sick. I've been caring for her, and now I need your help."

Natalie retreated and slumped into an armchair. "I gave that up," she said. Her facade melted, and tears overtook her.

"I know," said Tessie.

"I won't do it," said Natalie. "I won't." She swung from tearful to angry and back.

"You owe me," said Tessie. "You left me there!"

Natalie hunched forward, her head in her hands, silently sobbing.

"I'm out of money," Tessie said, "and out of options."

"You were always stronger than me," said Natalie. "I had to leave. I knew you'd be fine without me."

"Three days," said Tessie. "Three days is all I'm asking for."

"Why?" asked Natalie. "What's so important?"

"I have an opportunity," said Tessie. She explained how hard it had been to take care of her—their—mother, with no support. How dim the future looked. And Rob's letter and what the extra money would mean for her.

"I want to," said Natalie, "but I can't."

"You can," replied Tessie. "If I can, you can."

Natalie, the gleam gone from her eyes, looked like a half-deflated helium balloon.

"I thought you were done with all that television stuff," she said.

Tessie shrugged weakly. "Things don't always work out like you planned."

Chapter Three

Something felt wrong the moment Tessie opened her front door. Whether it was the air being extra still, or the scent lingering there being more sour, or the tingle prickling the nape of her neck, she didn't know; but she did know she needed to investigate quickly.

"Ma?"

Tessie tossed her keys on the end table and looked for her mother on the living room bed, but even in the darkness, she sensed the woman wasn't there. She flicked the lights on and confirmed her suspicion. The bed was disheveled, but barely looked like anyone had been lying in it.

"Ma!" Tessie said, louder this time.

She couldn't have gone far. Tessie wandered down the main hallway to the bedrooms. Still no reply, and no visible clues about where her mother had gone. She poked her head into her bedroom and saw nothing.

"No, not my den," she said softly to herself as she entered her private room.

Her mother lay on the floor there, wheezing, a dribble of vomit down the front of her flimsy nightgown. She stared at Tessie with hatred in her eyes. "Where's my clothes?" she spat. "I'm leaving."

Her mother had made threats before, but this was the furthest she'd gone to carry one out. Had she had a burst of energy? Had she become less rational—or more? She'd been getting increasingly desperate as her disease progressed, and Tessie's armchair psychiatry was less and less up to the task of understanding what her mother was thinking.

"Where would you go?"

"Anywhere but here," said her mother.

Tessie knelt to gather the skeletal figure, and her mother resisted, but her weak arms were no use. Tessie scooped her up; her mother stopped fighting. Back into the stuffy living room and into the small-but-roomy bed.

"Please stay here," said Tessie as she retreated to the bathroom to grab a warm washcloth and a fresh gown.

When she returned to the living room, her mother was half-asleep. She'd spent so much energy making it down the hall, then exerting herself against her daughter, that she had nothing left. Tessie removed the dirtied gown and wiped away the traces of bile on her mother's mouth and upper chest. The ruts between her ribs were deepening; the skin there was saggy and yellow. Her mother didn't resist, and Tessie barely noticed the natural inertia of a limb's weight. Manipulating her mother's body was like playing with a doll. Tessie pulled the fresh gown over her mother's head, smoothed it out, checked the bedclothes to ensure they, too, hadn't been soiled, and laid her back into the bed. She began gently snoring, and even Tessie's rearrangements didn't disturb her.

Tessie collapsed onto the couch across the room. She imagined maybe she wouldn't need Natalie's help because her mother would be dead soon, then browbeat herself for having such a thought. What did it matter—it wouldn't be long now, and she couldn't change things. Now that she'd set her heart and mind on reuniting with Rob for one last show, she half-expected her mother's last cruel act of defiance to be dying before she could get out of town.

Tessie found herself thinking of her visit to Natalie. She'd managed to get a peek at her niece. Though Anastasia hadn't woken, Natalie had relented, letting Tessie look into the little girl's room. Her hair had fallen across the crib in soft auburn curls, already long for a toddler.

For the second time in an hour, Tessie felt something wrong. She snapped to the present, searching for what unsettled her. Silence. Her mother had stopped snoring, and her chest seemed still. Her eyes weren't completely closed. Tessie leaned in to check for breath and perhaps jostle her, and the old woman's head jerked with a start, her eyes popping open. A flicker of red fleeted through her pupils, and then her eyelids fluttered and her mother was back.

"You were gone," said her mother. "Where did you go?"

Now was as good a time as any to break the news. "I have to leave for a few days." Her mother frowned. "You'll be taken care of."

"I don't need—"

"I know, I know, but you'll have company anyway." Tessie braced herself. "Natalie."

Her mother closed her eyes. So that was it. No argument, no rant. Nothing. Or maybe the calm before the storm. The silence wrapped itself around Tessie, and she couldn't stand it. When her mother opened her eyes again, her pupils were darker than black and tinged scarlet.

"Just abandon me like you did your father," said the old woman.

"He—," started Tessie. "No. We're not going through this again." She'd had no loyalty to that man. Tessie remembered him pounding on the door to her bedroom, threatening a beating (on behalf of her mother, of course), she and Natalie cowering behind their matched twin beds. He'd always been too drunk to follow through, but that didn't make the violent rattling of the door any less frightening.

When he'd died, she'd skipped the funeral, an unforgivable sin in her mother's eyes.

Tessie continued, "This trip will help us out. I'll make some money."

"You thought you'd be better than us, but you're worse," said her mother. "You're worse."

A headache began to erupt behind Tessie's eyes, and her energy for continuing the conversation was spent. "You'll get over it," she told her mother as she retreated to her den to pack for her upcoming trip.

Chapter Four

Tessie's mother hadn't said another word about the situation; or about anything at all. The silent treatment rated favorably on Tessie's scale of pain-in-the-ass-ness, given everything else her mother threw at her. When Natalie had first arrived at the house, she'd looked ready to flee, but Tessie had settled her in without incident.

Rob had emailed more information, and Tessie reviewed it on the plane. All-expenses paid to Podunk. Lucky her. Flying had never been her favorite part of the job, but these days she was out of practice, having managed to avoid planes since the show ended. An extra Xanax and some breathing exercises had helped the flight go without incident so far. She stared out the window—they were getting close now.

The man in the middle seat stole glances at her laptop—and at her—when he thought she was looking the other way. Maybe she should've bought a privacy screen. It didn't matter. There was nothing sensitive about the material, but she resented the intrusion. He formed a barrier between her and the aisle, and he made no effort to give her the space she was entitled to; the least he could do was keep his eyes to himself.

"Don't I..." Here it came. Tessie had changed her look since leaving the show: cut a few inches off her wavy brown hair, straightened it, wore it up more often. She'd lost a bit of weight—the very last remnants of her baby fat—giving her face a more angular appearance. The small changes along with a few years' age prevented people from noticing her as often.

But when she was looking at haunted houses on a laptop screen and her seat neighbor had three hours to observe her, it all went out the window.

"Don't I know you?" he asked.

"I... no, I don't think so," she replied, leaning away and turning her head, as if he hadn't already had a chance to study her. The landscape was still and black, though she could see the beginnings of lights toward the dark horizon.

"I'm sure I do," he continued. "You look awfully familiar."

Tessie straightened her shoulders, pushing against the man's bulk, and turned to look him in the face. "You're mistaken," she said. "I would remember. Please, I have work to do."

He looked abashed, and Tessie returned to reviewing the house's history. The Hardies were an interesting case. An upper-middle class family, five children, standard ghost sightings, eerie noises, and voices in their heads. Well, not all of them—just the wife and the two youngest children. The father, renowned for being—

"I *do* know you," said the man. "You were on television. You were on *Ghostshow*."

Tessie formed a smile she hoped looked less fake than it felt.

The man continued, his speech speeding up. "I almost couldn't place you. I should have known—I watched every episode. I can't believe I didn't recognize you immediately. You know what it was that did it? That cute little scar." His voice grew louder with each statement, and Tessie saw others on the plane turning towards them, craning their necks for a better view.

"I'm flattered," she said in a low voice, "but please, let me read in peace."

"I'm a fan," the man insisted. "Didn't you hear me, I've seen every episode." Something seemed to click into place behind the man's eyes. "Hey, I saw an ad for your special coming up... are you researching the house? Are you headed there now?" He seemed to be eating into more of her space, even though he was confined to his own seat.

"I can't talk about—"

"You can tell me," said the man, his voice now a loud low whisper, as if the conspiratorial tone would dissuade the rest of the passengers who'd begun observing the interaction. "I won't blab."

"I can't—"

"Is Rob on the plane?" asked the man. "Maybe I should ask him. He seems to know more anyway." An edge of malice bled into his voice. "Did you ever get tired of being wrong?" The last word hung in the air like the tolling of a far-off bell. He loomed over her, his body spilling into her space.

"Please leave me—"

"Were you ever right, even once?" he said, the question dripping with derision. "Remember the episode where you said there couldn't possibly be a Civil War ghost, and Rob—"

"Leave me alone!" shouted Tessie. The craned necks snapped back and people returned to minding their own business, pretending they'd never been interested in the first place, but the man wouldn't break his gaze.

He blinked seven times—four then two then one—and stared at Tessie for an eternity. His skin was marked with bumps of acne, pockmarks, and patches of hair pretending to be a beard; his eyes were dull. A red clot the size of a ladybug blemished the white of his left eye. Wisps of hair brushed his forehead, waving in the stale air expelled by the vent above his seat. He turned his concentration back to his in-flight magazine and grumbled, "Bitch."

"Is everything okay here?" asked a flight attendant with a plastic smile and pancaked makeup. The central aisle seemed miles away.

Tessie swallowed her anger, mumbled "Fine," and returned to her own business. The man continued to talk under his breath, loud enough for Tessie but no one else to hear. He was hate mail made flesh. She would need to tune him out for a while longer, so she turned her mind back to the show.

The special's producer, a goth named Xavier-but-call-me-X Johnson, had filled her in on the finer details. They were all set to air. It would be a live show for the first time in their history—a true event. A "one-time only" spectacle she knew would be repeated if the ratings were high enough. She had no intention of returning, though, ratings be damned.

Her computer dinged. New email. From the University of Maine, subject: admission.

The rejections from archaeology PhD programs had dribbled in over the last few days. She considered only schools that took her seriously; she'd turned down the ones looking to admit her as a publicity stunt, though the likelihood of that had decreased as *Ghostshow* faded from the public's memory.

Her hand hovered over her keyboard, and she hesitated to display the body of the email. Her heart raced. She tapped "Enter" and her screen froze. Nothing. She hit the key again, and again, speeding her tempo, but the screen stared at her, unchanged. Icons in the screen's corner depicted lost wi-fi connectivity and low battery power. The screen flashed and went out.

"Dammit," she whispered. She jiggled her computer, then shook it, like that would help. When it stayed dark, she slammed it against the tray table and barked a quiet "No!"

Tessie's mind flashed to an image of the Hardie House, and she found herself looking out the plane window once again.

Unintelligible whispers echoed in Tessie's head. She struggled to breathe. The earth below was dark, but she swore she could identify the exact spot where the house lay, and in response the house flashed its lights on; and there it was, a beacon in the expanse of darkness. Her vision telescoped and she saw the front yard of the house, the rotting white fence, the knotty trees, a mangy dog limping across the lawn, hopelessly chasing a squirrel. The house flickered between its two incarnations, seeming to somehow be both the craftsman and garrison at once.

The plane banked, leaning in toward the house. The man on her left side pushed against her, squeezing her against the hull of the cabin. He smelled sour. The fugue in her head morphed into sounds she comprehended: it taunted her, dared her to come closer, warned her to stay away. Her blood ran to her head and built pressure in her temples and eyes, until there was no blood anywhere else in her body and her skull would surely explode. Her nose began to bleed.

The lights dimmed and the plane shook with turbulence. It continued deeper into its bank, leaning at an angle close to perpendicular. The wing pointed at the ground, the man beside her was on top of her, crushing her; she fought to turn her head against the immense gravitational force pulling her—pulling them all—toward the house, and she saw the toll taken on the man, too. The clot in his eye grew and bulged until it was another eyeball, connected by the thinnest fistula, and it started leaking blood—drip, drip, onto her face—and Tessie gagged and gasped for air. The plane lights went out, and the house beckoned. Everyone screamed.

"Are you okay?" asked the man next to her, though it was more accusation than inquiry. Tessie glanced out her window—nothing but a few twinkling lights in the darkness. She'd been the sole person screaming, but near-silently, so only the stranger beside her could hear. She wiped her nose with the back of her hand, expecting blood, but coming away with only a trace of mucus.

Maybe the extra Xanax had been a mistake.

"I'm fine," she said. She straightened in her seat and returned her attention to her laptop, but its screen remained blank. The email would have to wait.

Chapter Five

X WAS WAITING FOR Tessie in the airport terminal. A bit older, hair still dyed black, facial jewelry in place, some new ink and a second lip ring. Cheekbones she'd kill for. Tall, gaunt, and dressed all in black to enhance the appearance. He broke into a smile as soon as he saw her.

"They roped you in, too, huh!" She ran to embrace him.

"Getting the whole crew back together," he replied. "We're a big deal, haven't you heard?"

X navigated through the terminal. Tessie fell behind as she powered her phone on, eager to read her email, but the device wouldn't comply.

"Dammit," she muttered.

"Everything alright?" asked X, slowing his pace.

"Are we headed to the hotel? I need to read an important email, and my phone's dead. Computer's dead, too."

"You need to manage your battery life better," said X. "Besides, what's more important than this?" He sped back up, Tessie needing two steps for every one of his. Damn long legs.

"They were fine, before," said Tessie. "I don't know how they died so quickly. Maybe I just lost track of time—I had this nightmare on the plane, seemed so real…"

X stopped and turned to face Tessie. His eyes were wide. "This house, right?" As if that were a reasonable explanation. X was more in Rob's camp than hers when it came to supernatural phenomena. Though he was complicit in the subterfuge, X considered himself to be a messenger helping the spirits be heard. "Anyway, sorry, no go for the hotel. Busy day filming tomorrow."

"Tomorrow?" asked Tessie. "I thought we had two days."

"Didn't you get—" said X, then looked at the inert phone in her hand. "I guess not. We've been moved up to accommodate the weather conditions."

"Weather? It supposed to be bad in two days?"

"Tessie, it's like you've forgotten everything," said X. "It's gonna be bad *tomorrow*. Thunder, lightning, the whole nine yards. Perfect spooky filming conditions." He elongated the middle o's in spooky and bobbled his eyes in their deep sockets. "The equipment's in the car, ready to go."

The meaning of X's words sunk in. "Jesus, that means we have to—"

"Yeah," said X. "Hope there's a late-night coffee place around here. We have a lot of work to do."

·········

Tessie's stomach sank at the thought of heading straight to the house without a solid night's sleep. She'd take even a short stay to recharge herself and her phone. She hadn't expected to have to deal with the house so soon, and she surely hadn't expected to be riding in a cramped '77 Ford Pinto.

"How'd we end up with this car?" she asked X. Her eyes burned, and the night's work hadn't even begun.

"Buddy of mine lent it to me."

"You and Rob and your buddies." No power adapter in the classic meant no chance to charge her phone. "We couldn't've rented a modern car like normal people?"

"Do I look like normal people to you?" X grinned and his lip rings glinted in the light of a passing streetlamp. "You look tired. We'll make a stop as soon as we see something open."

As if responding to X's declaration, a nondescript diner appeared on the left-hand side of the road. If Tessie hadn't been so focused on finding a place, she would have missed it. A small house with six windows across the front, split three and three by a standard door itself containing a half-window, it could easily be mistaken for a personal residence. Must've been grandfathered in before the zoning laws.

"Pull over," she said. "There."

X replied, "It's just a shack of a house."

"Look," Tessie said, pointing. The door's window held a faded black, white, and orange "Yes, We're Open" sign at a crooked angle, and over the door hung a piece of painted plywood proclaiming the establishment *The Greasy Knife*. A driveway wide enough for three cars abutted the building on its left-hand side. X swerved the car into a parking spot. The headlights illuminated a second, newer-looking section of the building attached to the rear; the structure as a whole looked like two halves of different houses rammed together at their corners.

The door opened not with the tinkle of a bell but the squeal of old hinges. The cafe's interior was better lit than Tessie had feared. She and X were the lone patrons. They chose a booth among a small bank of them lining the front wall. The counter guarded a dark doorway on the side wall leading to the newer part of the building. A bell jar imprisoned a half-dozen desiccated pastries behind a handwritten sign advertising "$3 each, 2 for $7."

"Nice choice," said X to Tessie with an eye roll. She unpocketed her phone and poked under the table for a place to plug in.

"You can use the outlet by the counter," came a gravelly voice from the doorway, "but we don't get no reception here. Never had it good beginnin', but the whole town's been out ever since the storms last week."

Tessie sighed. She'd never make it to that email. Popping up from the table, she took in the voice's owner: an older woman in a rust-colored gingham dress and a beige apron, with a name tag that said "Meggie" above her left breast. She might have been pretty once—or not—but she looked like life had gnawed her bones and sucked their marrow. The bags under her eyes threatened to swallow her face, and her limp hair was pulled into a loose ponytail, except for a brown-gray strand that fell over her right eye.

Despite her frazzled look, Tessie noticed a familial re-semblance in the woman. Smooth her wrinkles, add some color to her hair, straighten her posture, and she could've been Tessie's mother before she fell ill. Take thirty years off in addition, her sister—or herself.

"But we got a real phone out back," Meggie continued. "One o' them old ones, rotary. Substantial, not like these flimsy things everyone's got now." She squinted her eyes in what might have been a smile. "Sturdy 'nuff to kill someone with."

X stifled a laugh. Meggie tilted her head with a sudden movement and faced him. "Something amusing?"

"Sorry, tired is all," said X. Meggie nodded deliberately, her eyes fixed on X, and tolerated—but didn't accept—his apology. Tessie thought of all the times she'd served a jackass when all she was trying to do was scrounge tips to make ends meet.

"Can we get," said Tessie, her voice a squeak, "some coffee? Please?"

Meggie turned her attention to Tessie, and the older woman's unflinching glare reminded her of the man on the plane. "You wanna use the phone—" she jerked her head toward the dark doorway, "—or not?"

"No, no—I'm interested in email," said Tessie, but Meggie had turned around and walked to the counter after the first no.

X raised his eyebrows at Tessie. The smell of fresh coffee filled the air. Meggie remained behind the counter while the pot brewed, arranging and rearranging the supplies on the shelves, her back turned to the pair.

"I have to use the restroom," said X.

"Just leave me alone with the weird waitress," Tessie said. X gave her an apologetic shrug as he left the booth.

The window overlooked the dark street. The streetlights were sparse and dim, the moon covered by clouds. The heavy air weighed Tessie down. What was she doing? The trip had felt off from the beginning. Maybe it was her nerves about her future; maybe she was grasping at a chance to relive her past. Maybe she was out of practice.

That email was her future. Her shot at a new life. A real life. A life with distinction and respect and impact, not tawdry spectacle and reality junk food. She'd had fewer opportunities than Rob after *Ghostshow* ended—to be fair, she hadn't pursued that path—but if she wanted to return to television at a higher level than local commercials, this new special would reopen that world for her.

No, she couldn't think that way. Think positive: she'd be in graduate school soon, learning about ancient civilizations, maybe even getting the opportunity to participate in a true excavation.

X hurried to the table. "We need to leave," he said, sidling into the booth. He kept his voice barely above a whisper. He'd never been great at playing it cool. "There was dried blood on the bathroom wall."

"You're out of your mind, X. It could've been anything. How do you know it wasn't—"

"I know the difference between shit and blood," he replied. "This place gives me the creeps."

"I need caffeine," said Tessie. "There's nowhere else around. You'll be fine." She was used to X's overwrought emotions and paranoia before house prep. Every single time.

"But—"

"Cof-fee," replied Tessie. "And I'm hungry too."

"You're going to eat something from this place?" X's eyes widened. "You're braver than I remembered."

"Menus are on the table," said Meggie from behind the counter. "Coffee'll be out soon. I'm sorry our washrooms aren't to your likin'."

"Shit," said X.

The waitress continued, unfazed. "What's a pair like you doin' out here anyway? You're not local."

Tessie opened her mouth to reply, and X shot her a don't-you-dare expression. "We're here to investigate the Hardie House." X dropped his forehead into an open palm.

"Thought as much," replied Meggie. She wandered to the table and set down two mugs. Tessie inhaled the steam with a contented sigh. "Coffee. Well, you gonna order?" Irritation crept into Meggie's voice.

X shook his head. Tessie said, "Pancakes."

Meggie nodded and returned to the counter. Plasticware clunked as she gathered equipment before disappearing through the back door.

"You should've ordered something too," said Tessie. "You're going to be hungry. How big is this house anyway? Are we looking at an all-nighter?"

Talking about the house seemed to calm X down. "Not too bad," he said. "One main floor, and a half of a second. No attic, so that's good. No basement, either."

"No basement?" said Tessie.

"I guess they sometimes build on slab around here."

"Rob can't be too happy about that. Ghosts love attics and basements."

"We do have eaves."

"I hate eaves," said Tessie. "Too cramped. And there's mice." Tessie suppressed a shudder at the thought of the little beasts. "Much scarier than rogue spirits."

"We fear very different things, Tessie Gold."

Tessie glanced down at her phone and at the outlet. The floor between her and the counter seemed to stretch on forever, a linoleum chasm. Behind the table, she was cozy and safe, but out in the open, anything could happen. She tore herself from the comfort of her seat, strode across the void, plugged her phone in, and hurried back to the booth.

"What's that email you're so worried about?" asked X.

"Nothing important," said Tessie.

"You're a terrible liar."

"I'm waiting to hear from grad school," she replied. "Archaeology." She thought for a moment. "The real kind."

"What we do's not close enough?" X laughed. "Good for you. I'm sure—"

Meggie appeared at the table, plate in hand, and Tessie jumped. "I didn't even hear—" Meggie pushed the plate of pancakes toward Tessie.

"Pancakes," she said. Her eyes had gone white.

What had Meggie's eyes looked like when they first entered? She'd have remembered if they were only whites. Wouldn't she? Would she and X have even sat down?

X stopped blinking, and Tessie could tell he wanted to speak, or run, or both, but he sat there, paralyzed, Adam's apple bobbing and mouth open. He looked like a choking fish.

Meggie returned to the counter and Tessie noticed the knife tucked into the apron cord behind her left hip. X pointed emphatically toward the door, and in response, Tessie lifted her coffee mug. So the locals were a bit eccentric.

"Are you kidding me?" he hissed. "Did you fucking see that?"

"She probably has cataracts," said Tessie. Her voice wavered. "Besides, what do you think is happening?"

X rocked in his seat and drummed the table with his long fingers. Tessie no longer felt hungry. The current situation was more than a bit weird, and her strange dream on the flight didn't help. A thought gnawed at her, outlandish on its face: were Rob and X setting her up?

X pushed his coffee away and his rocking became more insistent. Tessie confronted her plate of pancakes to find they'd been drenched in syrup—and not good old-fashioned maple, but some red goopy abomination, artificial cherry or raspberry or, god forbid, strawberry. The melted butter floated on the surface of the syrup, shimmering like a colorful oil spill, its hue reminding her of the plane man's grotesque third eye. She retched involuntarily. X slid to the edge of the booth, but there stood Meggie, again from nowhere.

"Are my pancakes not to your likin' either?" she asked, her voice rising in volume. "Rude out-of-towners, come to gawk. Gawk, gawk. Maybe your parents never taught you manners."

"Fuck this!" said X and stood, but Meggie placed a palm on his chest, and with a gentle push, propelled him across his seat into the wall. The window rattled.

"Eat, Tessie," she said.

Tessie's body betrayed her. She stared into Meggie's clouded eyes, unable to look away. In the corner of her vision, she saw X's chest heave as he slumped against the wall, stunned from the aftermath of the waitress's shove.

"Do you need my help?" asked Meggie, almost playfully. "You need my help." She smiled a crooked smile. Her tone changed. "But I don't need your help," she said through clenched teeth.

Tessie couldn't make a sound. Meggie leaned over the table, reached across Tessie, and grabbed her fork, holding it tines down. Her left hand brandished the knife. She held the utensils at Tessie's eye level, Tessie stiff and trembling, mouth agape, a slow wheeze emanating from her windpipe as she willed herself to say something, to say anything, to move a finger or an eyelid.

Meggie lifted the fork and brought it down, piercing the soggy crimson pancakes and shattering the plate. "I don't need your help," she said, sneering. "But you need mine." A thread of blood—or was it syrup?—trickled from the corner of her mouth and her cheeks were pallid; she looked a corpse come to life, bearing little resemblance to the woman who'd greeted them when they entered the diner. She held up a triangle of soppy pancake, oozing red syrup and flecked with ceramic, and moved it toward Tessie's open mouth.

All Tessie's addled mind could think was: "Here comes the airplane."

A crash from across the booth broke Tessie's paralysis. X had smashed his elbow through the window. Meggie shrieked and started toward X. Tessie darted past the waitress. She glanced over her shoulder to see X halfway out the window, Meggie grasping at his feet. Tessie ran through the door and met X outside. She grabbed his arms and pulled with all her strength, and managed to drag him through the window. He'd lacerated the arm he used to break the glass, and the blood splattered on the dirt lot.

Meggie screeched through the broken window, and shards of glass painted translucent crimson framed her face. "I don't need your help!"

Tessie provided X an arm for support as they ran to the Pinto and then peeled out. "You didn't even drink your fucking coffee," he grumbled. The diner disappeared from the rear view mirror, but Meggie's wail echoed in Tessie's mind.

"Shit," said Tessie. "My phone."

"Get a new one."

"We need to go to the police," said Tessie. X's arm stained the upholstery red, though the bleeding had slowed. "And the hospital."

"No time," he replied. "We need to fix the house up. Tonight. Cast and crew are here tomorrow mid-morning and gone soon after."

Tessie shook her head. "But your arm—"

"I'm fine, and what are we going to tell the cop, that a possessed waitress tried to kill us?"

"A meth-head waitress."

X slammed the brakes and the seat belt bit into Tessie's neck and shoulder. She snapped back into the seat. "What the fuck is wrong with you, Tessie? Can you drop the skeptic act for a minute? What just happened was not natural."

"You know you get antsy before the houses," said Tessie, ignoring the queasy feeling in her own gut.

"This is different," said X. "What was she talking about 'helping'?"

"I don't know," said Tessie. She *did* know, though, that the waitress had sounded eerily like her own mother when refusing her pills or fighting to get out of the house. Without thinking, she mumbled, "Maybe the house doesn't need our help in making itself known."

X, already unnaturally pale, went even whiter. "The house doesn't want us setting up. Holy shit, that's it! We should forget it and find a place to spend the night—"

"Don't be ridiculous, we're setting up." Tessie sighed. She couldn't believe she was turning down the opportunity to get a good night's sleep.

"This fucking house." X was trembling; his arm was bloodied. If he and Rob had arranged the weird occurrences, X was committed to his part.

"Maybe you shouldn't believe this stuff," said Tessie.

"Maybe you should," replied X, and they drove to the Hardie House in silence.

Chapter Six

In person, the Hardie House looked dilapidated but otherwise average. The two lower front windows were broken, one containing a sorry-looking set of gray venetian blinds, the other simply empty. Paint was flaking off the clapboard. The shingles were warped; the moss-ridden roof probably leaked. Tessie found no remnant of the face formed by the doors and windows.

Her pulse had returned to normal during the car ride, though X remained flustered and wasn't speaking to her. He unpacked the trunk while she cased the property, noting any detail that could provide a narrative hook or a cheap thrill for their audience.

"How long has this place been abandoned?" she asked.

X remained silent.

"Goddammit X, get over it." He sulked as he piled the equipment on the sidewalk: prototype sensors, stage props, binoculars, a standard toolbox. Their cleverest trick involved granite dust. Tessie would sprinkle the powder over parts of the property, in creepy nooks and on creaky stairs, and during the show, they would use their patented Ecto-sensor™—in reality, a tricked-out Geiger counter—to "detect" the residue of a spirit. The ruse had worked well enough to fool Rob all those years. Every time the Geiger counter began to go crazy, so did Rob.

Tessie grabbed a flashlight and a pouch of granite dust and headed around the house to examine the yard. The house's side, a pentagon with a single small square window in the center, had less character than the front. Weeds poked their way through cracks in the foundation, and an ancient skim coat was now falling off in chunks. None of the disrepair displayed the unusual details necessary to make the show pop, though. Tessie kept looking.

A rotting wooden slat fence enclosed the house's small backyard, and a sparse copse of misshapen trees loitered beyond. Tessie passed through a rickety gate. It had locked at some point in the past but provided no security now. Moss and scrubby grass carpeted the uneven and pock-marked ground. Tessie's feet pressed into the yielding earth. It was like walking on a mattress. The flashlight dimly illuminated the treacherous contours of the yard, and Tessie concentrated to maintain her balance—the last thing she needed was to sprain her ankle. An ancient garden shed, in worse condition than the house, lurked in the back corner.

The gate swung closed behind her with a loud click. Tessie flinched and whirled around, expecting X behind her. The gate was unattended. Ground must be uneven. They could use that.

X's voice drifted in the air, strangely distant. *I guess he's talking to me again.* Tessie couldn't make out the words.

"Back in a minute," she yelled.

Tessie scoured the yard for any remarkable feature to work into the narrative. She discovered one near the shed: a deep hollow. She tested the ground with her toe and found it spongier than the rest of the yard. Likely the result of an old tree being taken down and the buried stump rotting over time, but by her telling, it would be an unmarked grave. Even better: a hidden entrance to heretofore unknown ancient catacombs under the house. She could manipulate the moss cover without it looking tampered with. If X helped, they might even be able to bury a prop to look like archaeological remnants of a mausoleum.

She'd be careful to provide little enough detail for viewers to disprove her theory with an instant internet search, but it didn't matter if they figured out the ruse after the fact. No one cared as long as they couldn't find the truth while watching the show. She sprinkled the granite dust around the area.

The familiar rhythms of exploring the house, developing a narrative to scare the hell out of the audience, and arranging the "proof" soothed her. It was equal parts art and science. Even the email felt less urgent now. The email! She couldn't believe she'd almost forgotten about it. Maybe she should stick to the reality TV business.

Tessie dismissed the thought. She'd never be taken seriously on her own merits being the foil on a stupid reality show. A raspy voice echoed in her head: *You'll never be taken seriously either way.* It sounded like the man on the plane. Like the waitress Meggie. Like her mother.

"Shut up," she said, and the phantasm went silent.

The shed beckoned her. She pushed its door open and revealed the darkness within. No windows let the scant moonlight enter, so she scanned the room with the flashlight: mostly empty, a rotting workbench covered with leaves and other detritus, silt and pebbles on the floor. Roots and chalk-pale weeds poked through cracks in the floorboards.

Finally, a perfect feature to figure into her tale. She just needed a story. Maybe it was built to hide the entrance to the catacombs, but the ground had shifted over time, revealing the opening to those who knew how to find it. That could work.

X's voice carried to her on the wind once again.

"Dammit, X," she said, leaving the shed behind and completing her circle around the far corner of the house. No X in sight. His voice was stronger now, the words still muddled.

Tessie peeked around the corner. A squad car was parked at a strange angle across the middle of the street, its lights turning the neighborhood into a cobalt and crimson nightmare. X was arguing with someone. Tessie angled herself to bring the other figure—a police officer—into view without giving herself away. They'd been concentrating too much on one another to have heard her talking earlier.

The cop stood uncomfortably close to X and pointed to the pile of gear on the sidewalk. X raised his hands in frustration. Tessie strained to hear the conversation, but despite their proximity, their voices came in waves and the words bled into one another, the audio equivalent of trying to read writing in a dream. The officer moved with the same herky-jerky motions as the waitress in the diner. Tessie's stomach clenched.

X reared back to throw a punch. Tessie yelled, "Don't do it!" as X's fist flew past the dodging police officer, who pushed X to the ground. X jumped up and the two men faced her. X's eyes pleaded with her. Tessie retreated, torn between helping her friend and saving herself.

"Run," said X.

A light flashed and a sharp crack echoed through the neighborhood.

X lurched forward, and the pale light of the streetlamp slanted across his brow, obscuring his eyes in deep shadow. His nacreous skin stretched taut across his cheekbones and forehead; his shiny spiky hair was oily and flattened against the crown of his skull. His mouth contorted into a rictus. A small patch on his chest became glossy and turned a shade darker than black, glimmering and grotesque and growing; under the sickly gleam of the yellow light, his shirt turned to satin.

Tessie ran.

Into the back yard, the spongy turf threatening to trip her with every step. Away from the lights of the street and the squad car. The spindly trees dancing in the mist offered no sanctuary, and the cop was coming for her next. Tessie didn't dare look behind her. *Go to the shed.* No, she couldn't, but she had no better option.

She snagged her foot in a divot, turning her ankle, and tumbled into the sweet moss, the soft ground blunting her impact. She crawled, her sneaker claimed by the pit, the rich soil finding its way deep underneath her fingernails. She vowed to never again make fun of those girls who tripped in horror movies.

The shed loomed in front of her, its dark maw open wide. She stumbled to her feet, the officer behind her, and she dashed for the shed. Her ankle exploded in pain. Reaching safety, she pushed the door closed behind her and barred it with her flashlight. She scrambled to the corner, hid under the rotting worktable, and waited. Her sole companions were her breath and the rush of blood in her ears.

The door rattled. The flashlight cast awkward stuttering shadows from its angle near the wall. The door rattled again; then silence. Unwanted thoughts of her father accosted her; for a moment, Tessie was back in her childhood bedroom. Then the flashlight flickered out, leaving her in complete darkness. She pulled her knees to her chest and pushed herself far into the corner of the room. The musty dampness of the once fragrant, now-moldy wood brought her mind back to the shed. Something grazed her neck, but Tessie was too shell-shocked to brush it away.

The image of X's twisted face filled her mind and her chest heaved with silent sobs. The raspy voice returned: *I don't need your help, but you need mine.* Tessie wanted to quiet it, to scream it into submission. Maybe X had been right about not setting the house up. Maybe it didn't need her help.

She no longer heard the officer outside, but how would she know when it was safe? Her ankle throbbed. When would the crew arrive? X was dead. X was dead! She swallowed, but the knot remained in her throat. She hugged her knees tighter.

She crossed her legs at the shins, placing her injured ankle atop her other foot, relieving it from the shed's dank floor. The elastic of her sock bit into her swelling calf. She removed it, relaxing the pressure. The dampness of the shed insinuated itself into her bones and she began to shiver. The more she tried to still her teeth, the harder they clanked against one another.

Without her phone, Tessie couldn't tell what time it was. The shed was tightly constructed for such a wreck; not a sliver of silver moonlight penetrated the structure, and the black remained as deep now as when the flashlight had blinked out. Her heart slowed and her breathing returned to normal, but her sadness grew. Her body ached like she had the flu. Her stomach growled, but Tessie felt more ill than hungry.

The liminal symphony of small sounds came into focus. The shed creaking in the gentle breeze. The dead leaves rustling on the floor. The spiders spinning their webs, and the mice skittering. The tiniest nose tickled Tessie's bare toes, but her ankle ached too much to kick the pest away. Claws scratched at her as the mouse climbed the mountain of her foot.

"Shoo!" she said, her voice a quiet hiss.

Another nose at her foot. And another. The squeaks multiplied. Mice covered her feet and fell onto her head from the workbench above. They made their way into her shirt and up the legs of her pants, and she wriggled, but they dug their claws in deeper. Squeaks filled her ears, and the door began to rattle and thump again. Tessie clenched her jaw to keep from squealing, and she brushed the mice away, but they continued to swarm her.

Then they began to bite.

Pinprick stings assailed her head and chest and feet and legs and blossomed into a full burn over her entire body, mice scratching and gnawing, finding their way through her tangled hair, a maelstrom of tails and claws and tiny teeth. Tessie erupted into a scream and convulsed, the blinding pain in her ankle be damned. She clawed at the mice as they clawed at her. A series of bangs shook the door, and the wood crackled and began to buckle. Tessie spun, flinging mice into the darkness around her. When the officer came through the door, she would make damn sure he got a faceful of rodents too.

"Tessie!" came a voice from the door. "Are you in there?"

X's voice. How could it be? A trick. The officer had stolen X's life and now his voice.

"Go away!" she yelled. She'd rid herself of most of the mice, but a stubborn one remained snarled in her hair above her ear, and she grabbed at the beast and pulled it away. Tessie directed all the emotion of the night into her fingers, the experience of the diner and seeing X killed, of the misfortune of the trip and the dead-end of her life—and she squeezed her hand with all her strength. The mouse screeched and bit her as its flesh exploded in her fingers.

"Let me in, Tessie!" said the voice. "I can hear you!"

The door crashed open and sunlight limned X's silhouette—a goth angel to the rescue. "Look!" she cried, thrusting the bloody mess in her hand toward X.

"What?"

Tessie's hand was empty. The shed, now pedestrian in the morning light, showed no evidence of mice.

"Who are you?" She retreated from X as he neared her.

"Tessie, what the hell happened to you? You're a wreck."

"I saw him, it—"

"Who?"

"I saw it shoot you. You're dead."

"I'm pretty sure I'm not dead, Tessie." He pirouetted like he was trying on a new black t-shirt and looking for opinions.

"Your arm," she said.

"What about it?"

"It's not injured any more."

"Tessie, you're not making any sense."

"The diner. The cop—"

"Yeah, nice guy," said X. His eyes lit up and he patted his front pocket. "He returned your phone. It's even charged. But let's get you to the hotel and cleaned up. We only have a bit of time before everyone else arrives. Can't have Rob spotting us with all of this shit. Would ruin the surprise."

Tessie stared at X.

"And please tell me you finished the setup," he said.

Chapter Seven

Dear Ms. Gold,

Thank you for submitting your application to the Archaeology Graduate Studies Department at the University of Maine at Bangor. We have carefully reviewed your materials and we regret to inform you that we will not be extending you an offer of admission at this time.

Every year we receive an increasing number of highly qualified candidates for a limited set of available spots. We are only able to admit a few applicants. We comprehensively review information we think will predict whether the applicant will be a successful student, including potential research opportunities and faculty fit.

In your case, it was overwhelmingly these last factors that played a role in our choosing not to admit you. Your unique background and interests do not conform with the kinds of research our department chooses to undertake, and we believe this misalignment represents an insurmountable barrier for your academic career with and beyond our institution. We appreciate your prior accomplishments in a non-academic field, but we do not feel it will translate into academic success in archaeology.

If you have any questions, please contact the admissions office. Do not contact the Department of Archaeology. If your situation changes or you believe yourself to be a better candidate in the future, feel free to reapply, but you will not be given any special consideration as a repeat applicant. We wish you best of luck in your present and future endeavors.

Sincerely,

Stephen Barker

Dean of the School of Social Sciences, University of Maine

....

The rejection read the same after Tessie's shower as it had before. She scrolled up and down on her phone, as if the words would magically change when they reappeared on the screen. If it had been paper, she'd have ripped it to pieces, but she'd spent enough time without her phone on this trip to damage it out of anger.

Insurmountable barrier. Didn't sound like something that would be overlooked the next time she applied. Or the time after.

And what would her mother say? Tessie could always not tell her mother the news, but the old woman would know. She always knew, somehow. And she would gloat—Tessie could hear the "Told ya" as if her mother stood in the plain, small room with her.

She and X had struck out on finding anything fancier than the no-frills roadside motel, but the proprietor hadn't tried to kill them, so Tessie considered it a net win. The walls and furniture and carpet retained the faint scent of cigarette smoke and bleach, like someone had tried to chase out the smell, but despite their best efforts it lingered.

Tessie tossed her phone onto the bed and towel-dried her hair. She needed to find a way to survive the day. By some miracle her ankle was not severely injured; what she had thought a major sprain turned out to be a minor ache. A faint bruise blemished the pale skin around the knob of her ankle, but it accepted her full weight without so much as a twinge of pain.

The ordeal had left Tessie little time to prepare for today's shoot. Her bag of granite dust remained distressingly full, and unless X had planted some props, she'd have nothing to riff off. This show was going to require her best effort—and being broadcast live would require even better. *Ghostshow* was all she had left now.

A knock came at the door. "Ready?"

X hadn't been much help figuring out the previous night. The cop had checked what they were doing, ensured the permits were in order, and returned her phone; X had finished unloading the equipment and then looked for her to no avail. He'd assumed she'd been exploring some cranny of the house, and so he'd settled into the back seat of the Pinto and closed his eyes. Next thing he'd known, it was morning. That's when he'd realized she was still missing and he'd found her screaming in the shed.

She'd asked him about the diner and his arm, but he'd remained curiously close-mouthed on the subject. He'd submitted to her demand to examine his arm—thought it funny, even—and she'd found nothing but the flawless chiaroscuro of black ink and translucent skin.

The door rattled harder this time. "C'mon Tessie, time to go!"

"Give me a minute," she said as she unlocked the two deadbolts, unfastened the chain, and popped the door-knob lock. Tessie wasn't sure if four locks made her feel more secure or less.

X stood there, a coffee in each hand, looking exactly as he had the previous night when he picked her up at the airport. Color and body had returned to his cheeks, his hair was spiky, and his eyes sparkled. He was certainly enjoying this trip.

"You look a hell of a lot better," he said. "Make-up artist will get you the rest of the way there." He grinned.

"Thanks," replied Tessie, part sincere, part sarcastic. She felt a hell of a lot better, truth be told. "Coffee!"

"You were so excited about it last night," said X. "And you didn't even get a sip."

The previous night's memories were hazy, like they'd been filtered through a dream. The ordeal with the waitress hardly seemed real. Her time in the shed was sharper—if she concentrated she could feel the mice crawling all over her—but she had no outward signs of bites or any evidence otherwise to corroborate her version of events.

"X, what's going on?" she asked as they walked to the Pinto. Too bad she hadn't hallucinated *that* shitbox.

"We're going to meet Rob at the house?" X said, like he was answering a trick question.

"You know what I mean," said Tessie.

"I'm not sure I do," he replied, "but I'm guessing you want to talk more about last night. I told you what I remember."

X started the Pinto up. Tessie had a few short minutes to start X talking before they arrived at the Hardie House.

Tessie exhaled. "Something weird is going on."

"You don't believe in weird goings-on," said X. He meant nothing by it, but his tone aggravated her.

"The diner? The waitress? You going through the window?" She shook her head, looked away from X and back. "The cop shooting you? Where do you want to start?"

"Whoa, slow down," he said. "We've been through this. The waitress was—" His phone buzzed in his pocket. "Hold on, it's probably Rob." X plunged a hand down his front jeans pocket, fishing for his phone, and the car listed into the opposing lane. The road curved off before them. Tessie reached for the wheel, but X swatted her away, mouthing "I got it," and in the process swerved the car further left. X fumbled with his phone as he tried to right the car using his off hand and knee. Guard rails had appeared on both sides of the road.

X jolted the car into the proper lane as he put the phone to his ear and shot Tessie an apologetic look and a sly smile. "Rob! You there already?"

X and Rob's conversation held no interest for Tessie. She reclined her seat and stared through the sunroof. True to the weather report, the sky had started to film over, the wispy cirrus clouds giving way to their clumpy, more menacing stratocumulus cousins. Sunlight streaked through the edges of the lumps, highlighting the contrast between the frilly white fringes of the clouds and their charcoal interiors. The army of the gray was on the move, inexorably conquering the entire sky. The air took on a sickly shade of green.

"Everybody's here," said X. Tessie snapped out of her reverie as he slammed the Pinto to a stop. The crew surrounded the house like ants attacking a wad of chewed bubble gum. X hopped out of the car and joined a conversation with the production designer. Tessie scanned the crowd and tried to place the familiar faces she'd forgotten. So many unfamiliar ones. Rob was nowhere in sight.

Tessie unbuckled her seat belt, her fingers brushing the central console of the Pinto's front seat. The carpet felt clammy. Tessie's fingertips were flecked with half-dried blood. She studied the console; several rust-colored patches stained its tan carpet where X would have laid his bloodied arm the previous night. Tessie prodded at the spots. They were slightly damp, their edges crusted over.

A thump came from the side of the car, and Rob made goofy faces at her through the window.

"Jesus!" she yelped. "If anyone startles me one more time…"

Rob laughed. "Come on out of there," he said.

Tessie wiped her fingers on a clean swath of carpet. She swung the car door open, forcing Rob to jump out of the way or be flattened. She shot out of the Pinto. "Are you fucking with me?" she said, advancing on her co-star like a boxer stalking a staggered opponent.

"Nice to see you too, Tess," said Rob, retreating. Tessie followed.

"Cut the shit," said Tessie. "What are you and X up to?"

"Tessie." Rob held his palms toward her in a gesture of peace or surrender—maybe both.

Tessie paused her approach and examined Rob. He had superhero looks—square jaw, piercing blue eyes—and if he could act a whit, he'd have been a Hollywood leading man. The intervening four years had done nothing to take the shine off his prettiness; in fact, a bit of salt and pepper in his stubble and a few well-placed worry lines on his face gave him an air of gravitas that would change the character of his performance on the show. Given his boyish charm, Tessie wasn't sure if it was for the better.

"You're going to tell me everything," she said.

"I don't know what you're talking about," said Rob, "but I understand we have a lot to discuss."

"We do," Tessie agreed. "I've got something to check on first."

Rob opened his mouth to reply, but Tessie had already jogged off towards the front corner of the house where X collapsed the prior night. The crew parted as she neared. Those who didn't know her stayed out of her way; those who did had no time to offer more than a "Hey, Tessie."

"Right here," she said to herself. She knelt in the damp grass, brushed the yellow blades aside, and scanned for evidence. The crew had stampeded around the property, amateurs at a crime scene, destroying any hope of finding the telltale indentation. Dew had cleaned the grass. Tessie dug her hands into the ground, brought her dirt-covered fingertips to her nose, and sniffed, searching for the scent of iron, or anything else to validate her memories, but she smelled only earth, like the air before a rainstorm.

Chapter Eight

The crew had set up a table and chairs in the dusty kitchen of the house—a makeshift war room for the production, where they could plan the shoot and map out the day's activities. Gray sunlight streaked into the room through the tarnished windows and motes of dust danced in the dull rays. Work lanterns in the corners of the room reflected an artificial orange light.

"Guys, we need the room," said Rob. Two crew members chatting in the corner grumbled and exited through the rear door.

"I'm worried about you," he continued. When Tessie objected, he gestured at her hands, filthy from digging for evidence. "I need you on top of your game for today. Talk to me."

Tessie recounted the previous day's events as she best remembered them. Even now, her mind clouded over, and the words tasted false. She wouldn't have believed any of it were she in Rob's place, but he nodded his head and creased his brows at all the right times. Nothing she said fazed him. The bastard knew. He'd set everything up.

"Not me," said Rob. "Why would I trick you? It's the house."

"The house," she repeated.

"How much have we seen, Tess?" said Rob. "The evil in this one is strong. I'm worried for us both. The crew. We don't need bad mojo following us after this shoot. And if it's already started with you—"

Tessie couldn't keep it in any more. She stood up. "It's all fake, goddammit!" she yelled.

A crew member from the other room said, "Oh shit." X bounded to the door and ran his hand across his throat, his wide eyes betraying panic.

Tessie thrust her finger at her partner-in-crime. "Get the hell out of here. You're a part of this too, and I'll deal with you later."

"But—" X pleaded. Tessie took two heavy steps towards him, her teeth gritted. "So help me god, X, I will end you."

X clamped his mouth in defeat and left her alone with Rob once again.

Tessie turned to Rob. "It's all fake. We set this shit up ahead of time to make it look good. It's fake."

Rob sat in measured silence. He stood and suddenly towered over Tessie. The pale light in the room washed out his features. His smile disappeared and his eyes darkened. "You think I don't know?" It was only partially a question.

"What?"

"I've always known what's real," said Rob. "And what's not."

"And you figured a bit of turnabout would be—"

"No," said Rob. "I'm telling you: it's this house. It's not in your character to believe, but the phenomena are real. The previous spirits were real, too, even if you didn't notice what was happening."

Tessie's head swam. She fought to find a retort, but none materialized. Rob's faith was strong as ever. He worshiped this stuff. He'd never debase himself by playing pranks on her, even in retribution for her deceitfulness. She collapsed onto the flimsy folding chair and began to sob.

"You'll make it through this." Rob seemed back to his normal size. He placed a hand on her shoulder.

"It's more than this," she said. "It's my future. No grad school will ever admit me."

"I don't think that's true," said Rob.

"It was my last chance."

Rob laughed softly and shook his head. "Tessie." He moved his folding chair next to hers and wrapped his arm around her shoulders. She leaned against him, her head hanging. "Of course it wasn't. You'll keep trying, and you'll succeed. If not this way, then some other."

"You don't know," said Tessie. "This show is a curse."

"You're right, I don't know," replied Rob. "And maybe this show is a curse. Spirits haunt us in more subtle ways than moving chairs when we're not looking or tricking us into seeing things that aren't there." Tessie lifted her head. Rob looked out into the distance, at something only he could see.

He continued, "Maybe they're being good to us, even if it doesn't feel that way. Maybe they're trying to atone for wrongs they committed while living, or redeem themselves for all they regret not doing." He turned to Tessie, his eyes refocusing, and gave her a gentle squeeze. "Maybe they're trying to scare us away from the same mistakes they made."

Tessie blotted a tear with her shirtsleeve. Rob produced a tissue from nowhere. She yearned to believe in the supernatural in that moment, if it meant Rob's speech were true. "Do you really believe that?" she asked.

"I do," he said with a conviction Tessie wished she still felt for anything. A twinkle returned to his eye. "C'mon, Tess. Let's put on one hell of a show tonight!"

....

The clouds continued to roll in, and the day was overtaken by doldrums and a light mist. Thunder rumbled in the distance, but the spectacular lightning show Tessie expected hadn't yet materialized. Behind the cloud cover, the sun began its slow descent. Showtime loomed.

Wardrobe had gotten their hands on Tessie, and after cleaning her up, they provided her a cropped suede jacket to wear over her blouse and dark blue jeans. They passed her off to the makeup artist, one of the many new faces on set. Marta, if Tessie had heard correctly. She looked barely out of her teens. Tessie settled into the chair; this aloof child began to apply foundation to her. The cosmetics felt heavy on her face, a mask threatening to suffocate her.

Quiet hung in the air between them. Tessie shifted in her seat.

"Stay still," said Marta. She had a trace of an Eastern European accent.

"Sorry," said Tessie. "You been working with Rob long?"

"Few months," she said, not even feigning interest in Tessie's attempt at small talk.

Marta applied the next layers to Tessie's face in silence. She was all business as she brushed and powdered and dabbed, her own face rapt in concentration. The girl's eyes were such a dark brown they appeared all pupil and no iris, black holes that swallowed Tessie in their vastness and chilled her in their emptiness.

Marta took a step back and gave Tessie a once-over. "Almost done," she said, returning a brush to her kit and retrieving a skinny eyeliner pen. "Boy," she said with a smile, eyeing the pen, which in the slant light looked almost like a needle-thin dagger, "you really needed my help."

"What did you say?" said Tessie.

"Now hold as still as you can," said Marta, one hand grabbing the top of Tessie's head and the other thrusting the pen toward her eyes.

"No." Tessie grabbed Marta's wrist and held it steady. "We're done here." Marta tried to pull her wrist away, but Tessie firmed her grip.

"Suit yourself," said Marta as she wiggled her shoulders to free her hand. "You're crazy. Let me go!" Tessie pushed Marta's wrist and rose from the chair. It was time to find Rob.

"We still need to cover that scar of yours. We film in HD now!" called Marta after her.

"I look fine," said Tessie.

Rob stood in the front yard of the house, chanting under his breath, eyes closed, hands folded in front of him. This was new. For all his belief in the supernatural, Tessie never knew him to be religious; by all appearances, here he was invoking a higher power.

"Rob?" she prodded, afraid to interrupt his ritual.

He opened his eyes and smiled. "How are you feeling?"

"Where'd you find that makeup girl?" said Tessie.

"Don't mind her," said Rob.

"We'll start in the backyard," said Tessie. "Just like we talked about. The shed and those sad-looking trees will establish the atmosphere, and then we can circle back to the interior of the house."

Rob replied, "The spirits will guide us from there."

"Sure," said Tessie.

The crew congregated around the two stars. The cameramen and mic operators took their places; the director checked the lighting. Tessie scanned the throng of workers for X, who usually stood just off-camera, but she couldn't find him. The mist had thickened, the thunder had quieted, and still no lightning. The house looked mundane—nothing more than a woebegone structure in need of loving care from a new family.

The director signaled two minutes to Tessie and Rob. Tessie's stomach clenched, but it would settle once they started their banter. A sense of déjà vu gripped her.

"Anything last minute I should know about live TV?" asked Tessie.

"Whatever happens," replied Rob, "go with it."

"We're live in 3… 2… 1…" The director pointed at Rob and Tessie. The tally light flared red. On cue, a streak of lightning split the sky in half, and its associated peal of thunder followed, sharp and loud enough to set Tessie's ears ringing. The acrid smell of ozone mingled with the smoky scent of charred wood. The hairs on Tessie's forearms stood straight, electrified, and she wondered if the haunted grove was down a tree.

"Welcome back, ghost hunters! We've missed you," said Rob, his eyes wide. "We've got a treat for you today. We're here—live!—at the Hardie House…"

Tessie surveyed the crowd behind the camera looking for X. When the time came to use the Ecto-sensor or other ghost-hunting gear, he would jump into the frame to provide it. She and Rob never let him say much, though he always tried to squeeze in an extra word. He inspired a following even more dedicated than Rob and Tessie's, despite—or maybe because of—his meager on-camera time. It wasn't like him to miss an opportunity to ham it up.

"Tessie!" Rob wore an expectant look on his face.

"Um," she started. Rob's eyes narrowed. Tessie snapped to. She needed to artfully lead Rob to the back yard, to the places she'd set up.

Or did she need to be artful after all? Where had her art, her skepticism gotten her? Doing all the work, looking like an idiot, still being blacklisted by graduate schools. Maybe she could play the believer too.

"Rob, I think we should start back here," she said, recovering. Rob looked relieved. She needed to focus; post-production wouldn't be able to save her. No more slip-ups. She continued, "Have you seen this place? I was exploring this morning, and I think we're going to find some curiosities. Maybe some"—she cleared her throat—"actual spirits."

Rob registered mild shock and then self-satisfaction as he said, "Why, Tessie, I didn't expect that from you!"

"I'm full of surprises," said Tessie.

She and Rob retraced her path around the side of the house, with the main cameraman and someone Tessie didn't recognize both in pursuit, a motley procession through the rickety gate. The mist gave way to a cold rain, light but steady. Tessie led the entourage to the area near the shed, and she and Rob found their spots. She waited for the gravity to close the gate on its own—her first flourish—but the gate stubbornly remained open. The perils of live TV.

"What are we looking for, Tessie?" asked Rob, playing into Tessie's newly adopted role. "Where would the presence be the strongest?"

Tessie turned to face the camera. The tally light—usually a constant red eye in the darkness—flickered, then blinked. It reminded her of something; where had she seen four, two, one? The repeating pattern nauseated her and made her feel claustrophobic, and the camera lens grew in its rounded square case, intruding into her space, and she saw her reflection in the camera—old and haggard, and hadn't she seen that face before, in the diner? And the likeness laughed at her—she was betraying herself, somehow, and what was her name anyway, Tessie or Meggie, and whom did she serve? The lens opened its maw and swallowed her, and time stopped as she swapped places with her elder doppelgänger.

Tessie floated behind the lens of the camera, trapped and formless, a wraith watching her reflection made flesh and standing in the overgrown yard. Rob had disappeared. Old Tessie ran the show, solo.

"Hello, kiddies," she croaked, her voice gravelly and worn. "We're here at the Hardie House. Those of you old enough may remember our trip here decades ago: *Ghostshow Live!* That one didn't go so well." She winked at the camera, a gesture Tessie knew was for her sole benefit.

"You want to see some real spirits this time, don't you?" She smiled like a fiend, her teeth yellow and cracked and rimmed in rot. "A bona fide fucking demon. Well, do we have the torments for you!"

You can't say that on TV, thought Tessie.

"I can say whatever the fuck I want, honey," said the hag, tilting her head. She was talking only to Tessie now. "And I can do what I want. You, well... you're too pathetic to do what you want. You'll always be too pathetic."

The hag returned to addressing the imaginary audience: "You're looking for a demon who'll reach right through the screen and rip you open." She thrust a long-clawed hand out; Tessie no longer possessed a body, but she felt icy talons pierce her abdomen and wrench out her intestines. She screamed in pain but made no sound.

Then she realized she was no longer alone in the camera.

Her head filled with the voices of viewers watching this return trip to the Hardie House. *Look at that old hag. She's heinous.* Tessie willed herself to look around, as if she could see the source of these phantom voices, but she had no control over her field of vision. The TV screen was her world now. The voices echoed in her head. *I can't believe she's still doing this show.* Her doppelgänger laughed. *The guy was so much better.*

"Why else would you watch this show?" continued Old Tessie. "You want to be here, among the spirits, feel their presence. Let the Devil himself take his very best shot at you." She spoke with the same manic energy as Rob.

Change the channel. The space around Tessie compressed and created a gentle pressure that forced together her pain, increasing its density. *This bitch sucks. She's such a fraud.* The pressure intensified, crushing Tessie. Her phantom lungs itched, ached for oxygen, and the voices increased in volume, running into and over one another, a cacophony of venom directed at her. *She doesn't know anything. Get the guy back. This show is such trash. Was it ever any good?* The itch in her lungs blossomed into a starburst of agony, a flat, even pain contrasting with the dagger in her gut.

"This house is spectacular," said Old Tessie, her voice transforming from crackly to shrill, splitting Tessie's skull. "We're letting the demons loose with this one. Better turn off your TV before you're damned like the rest of us. Damned like me!" She cackled.

If Tessie could have fainted from the pain, or from the lack of oxygen, or from bleeding out of her gut, she would have, but fainting was not an option. She endured. But she wished for death. For more than death—for non-existence. She cursed her mother for bringing her soul into this world. Even if she escaped her camera-jail, she'd be returning to the future on display: old, worn out, wretched, a reality show hack. The raspy voice returned: *Now you're getting it.*

"What are we looking for, Tessie?" asked Rob. "Where would the presence be the strongest?"

Tessie gasped, inhaling the soggy air like it was her last breath, relishing her full lungs. Her hand had unconsciously moved to her stomach, and she felt around to make sure she was uninjured. Although the pain was gone, its shadow remained. The tally light provided its constant red illumination.

Rob looked impressed. "What happened?" he asked. "Did you sense something?"

"I..." said Tessie. "I need the Ecto-sensor."

Rob motioned to someone off-camera, another unfamiliar face—all the faces were unfamiliar now, except for Rob—and Tessie found the Ecto-sensor in her hands. She switched it on. The Geiger counter spat its staccato static, which varied with the smallest movement of the device.

As expected, it became louder and more rapid as Tessie approached the area by the shed.

Rob followed Tessie who followed her trail of granite dust. "I don't know if we've gotten such a strong signal in the entire history of *Ghostshow*. This is going to be something big!" His voice trembled with anticipation.

"Here," said Tessie, stopping at the edge of the hollow. The Geiger counter squealed as she turned it off. The sudden silence brought her to her senses—she hadn't prepared anything under the moss cover, and neither had X, from his account of the previous night. The rain worsened, and the spongy turf of the yard had softened further.

Time to make some shit up, thought Tessie.

"Guys, can you get this?" She waved the camera operators over.

"Tessie, what is it?"

"I'm not positive," said Tessie, "but from the size of this indentation, it could be an unmarked grave."

She realized her mistake a heartbeat before Rob said, "Let's dig."

The same production assistant who'd provided the Ecto-sensor handed spades to Tessie and Rob. Water pooled in the hollow. Rob dug with gusto, flinging clods of mud over his shoulder. Tessie excavated the opposite side of the indentation.

"Why would no one have noticed this before, Tessie?" asked Rob between shovelfuls. Dirty water and moss splashed everywhere in his zeal to uncover some morbid secret.

Tessie nodded toward the shed. "My theory," she said, "is the shed migrated as the ground settled. It concealed this, once upon a time."

A peal of thunder crackled overhead, lazily blooming into a full fledged rumble.

"And never underestimate the restless dead's will to be rediscovered," she added. Ten minutes into her new believer role, and she was already starting to sound like Rob.

Tessie pushed her shovel into the ground and—thunk. "Did you hear that?" said Rob, his excitement rising. The cameras moved in to catch a closer view of Tessie's handiwork.

Rob postured for the camera. "Time to get dirty. Don't let anyone tell you this isn't a real job." He tossed the shovel aside, knelt in the puddles, and clawed at the remaining moss cover with his hands. "Come on in Tessie, the water's fine!"

The cold rain had soaked through Tessie's clothes, and her bones ached. Pain echoed in her abdomen and lungs and head. She had no real desire to dive into the muck to uncover a bunch of nondescript rocks. *Whatever happens, go with it.* Live television afforded no time to discuss with Rob the merits of not becoming a muddy, soggy mess when they still had two hours of shooting before them.

Tessie braced herself and knelt. The mire oozed through her jeans, and its clammy fingers wrapped themselves around the backs of her knees, seizing her, inviting her to become part of the earth. The hollow could forever be hers. Maybe a ghost hunter or archaeologist would dig her up, and she would haunt the fuck out of them.

They cleared the mossy sludge from the hard surface below. The underlying structure came into view. At least Tessie hadn't sacrificed her favorite pair of jeans for nothing. She swept aside layers of mud with her open palms, revealing more of the stone slab. The camera hovered over her shoulder. The slab's surface held no epitaph—no words of any kind—but only two diagonal lines carved from corner to corner, a St. Andrew's cross.

Had they made an actual archaeological discovery?

"We're going to need help," said Rob.

Two burly crew members flanked Tessie, and with Rob, they dug their fingers under the edge of the slab and lifted. It was excruciatingly heavy, even with the help, and Tessie's back ached as she tried to do her part. The slab lifted two feet off its base, then stopped as the crew reached the limits of their strength; Rob croaked "On three! One more good heave!" and—three!—the slab fell over the far side, but Tessie lost her balance and tumbled forward.

She stared at the desiccated profile of X, features caught eternally in shock, skin pale and shiny as the night the cop had shot him; she screamed and tried to crawl out of the coffin, but something held her: the muck had grown arms. Roots and underground vines grasped her. An unnatural grin twisted X's face, and he stared at Tessie with milky eyes.

"You left me," he said through an unmoving mouth.

"You told me to run," said Tessie. "You told me."

"You left me," repeated X, angrier. The tendrils tightened their grasp on Tessie. "We were a team, and you left me to die."

Tessie had run out of things to say.

A sound like a thousand knuckles cracking filled Tessie's ears, and X's head rotated slowly to face her. His smile transformed into a grimace. Tears of blood beaded at the corners of his eggshell eyes.

"Why?" he asked, the word drawn out in agony. "Why did you leave me?"

"I didn't," said Tessie, tears in her own eyes. "I didn't know what to do."

"Why did you leave me to die, Tessie?" X sounded like a scared little boy. "You left me. Alone." No anger remained in his voice; only melancholy.

"Help me," said Tessie, to no one in particular. She clawed at the roots, disentangling herself, but the muck's fingers were not so easily removed. When one dissolved under her grip, another formed. Mud covered her hands and arms and splashed into her face; she tasted the earth and smelled it, heard it, the subtle sound of sand shifting, and it swallowed her.

The ground opened beneath them and they fell into an undiscovered sepulcher. The two of them landed in a coffin of her own making, surrounded by cold stone alcoves filled with the bones of the aggrieved. Restless, chattering, bitter bones. Centuries eroded Tessie's will to struggle; X went silent, his skin tautening further, rice paper over a delicate skull. The chill of the grave soaked into Tessie, and the cold infiltrated her so thoroughly it wrapped around to warmth. The taste of iron and chalk. *I'm sorry*, thought Tessie; *too late, too late*, she heard in return. Season after season, decades, epochs spent in quiet contemplation of all that she'd never done, all that she'd never been. The walls of the mausoleum crumbled, slowly, battered by time, and the other skeletons fell away, buried completely; X's grasp dissolved and he crumbled to dust, leaving Tessie disturbed and alone, except for the worms tickling her bones as they navigated the surrounding dirt.

Here she would lie, forever, in the sweet soft ground. No, she couldn't give up. A flash of mottled blue, like the ocean...

And a hand grasped her wrist. Pulled.

"Get out of there, Tessie," came a voice she'd last heard an eternity ago. Rob lifted her out of the pit, and she remembered she wasn't exquisitely dead, but a live TV show host, and they were filming even now. Lifetimes had passed with her in the ground, yet here she was, seconds since she first fell into the trench.

"She's fine, folks," said Rob to the camera. "Occupational hazard when you hunt ghosts." Rob never broke persona. Tessie had been in the land of the dead for so long, and Rob? He mugged for the camera.

"And nothing down there to boot," said Rob. He shook his head and sighed. "I thought we were onto something."

Tessie raised her hand to object, but looking into the pit and seeing nothing but slick mud, rocks, and jagged roots, she stayed silent. Rob looked for a hook he could build off. The rain quickened and washed the outermost layer of grime off Tessie. She shivered uncontrollably as the grave's chill bloomed in her.

"Let's get inside," Rob said to the camera and the crew equally.

A crowd of strangers—so many strangers—hustled Tessie into the house. Rob followed, nattering at the camera and trying to make the best of a rapidly deteriorating situation.

"She must have seen something," he said. Tessie sensed an undercurrent of concern in his voice, subtle enough to be undetectable to the viewers. She'd come this far; she wanted to continue, to show this entity it would not dissuade her. *Still not learning*, said the raspy voice.

The crew sat her down in an interior room. A small battery-operated space heater whined in the corner. Tessie rediscovered warmth, generated from fire and life, and reality sharpened for her, though she was no longer sure which was dream and which was wakefulness. Perhaps all of it was real, or none of it. Perhaps it didn't matter.

"Tessie, did you have an encounter?" asked Rob. His eyes betrayed his anxiety. "Can you tell us about it?"

"I did," she replied. She paused for effect. Her inner skeptic was rising, unwilling to be kept down any longer. "My head encountered those rocks at the base of that goddamned pit." *God has nothing to do with it.* "Knocked me for a bit of a loop, but I feel better now." The house would no longer unnerve her. She had a part to play and she was going to play it; she'd give no more recognition to the demon tormenting her. *I don't need your help.*

Rob looked crestfallen but relieved. "Can you go on?"

"Yes," she said. *No.*

"I have an idea," said Rob. "I noticed some bulkhead doors while we were outside. That means there's a basement." He turned to the camera and grinned. "I love basements."

"I thought this place didn't have a basement."

"You didn't find one earlier today?" asked Rob.

Tessie shook her head.

"Let's find out."

Tessie tore herself from the swell of warm air and joined Rob to scour the house for access to the basement. Most of the frames held no doors, and the few that did led to claustrophobic closets strewn with dust and debris: old cracked buttons, loose mounting nails, shreds of faded wallpaper. The cameraman followed Rob and Tessie as they reopened every door in the house. Tessie half-expected one of the closets to have transformed into a stairwell; then she reminded herself she was the skeptic.

Rob pattered on as they explored. "Basements are hotbeds of paranormal activity," he said.

"Why is that, Rob?" asked Tessie.

"Closer to the ground," he replied. "The dead know they belong there, back to the dirt that made them, and they long to be one with the earth, even if they don't consciously realize it."

Tessie yearned to run outside and hurl herself into the pit, to allow the warmth of the grave to reclaim her. To sleep the deepest sleep. She belonged in the ground now.

No—this wasn't her talking. She shook the thought off.

"Why aren't underground parking garages filled with inconsolable spirits?" she said.

"So flippant, Tessie," said Rob, shaking his head. "Here I thought you were coming around. Always the skeptic."

"Forever, Rob," she replied. *I'll show you forever.*

They found a slatted door in a corner of the kitchen, down a rear hallway Tessie hadn't previously noticed. A hallway she was certain hadn't existed the day before.

"Ladies first."

Tessie pushed the door open to find an ancient cast-iron boiler, half-corroded, dust hanging like Spanish moss off its byzantine pipework. Behind the boiler was another door, shorter and shabby. Tessie marched on, the cameraman following her; they pushed Rob aside, as the space fit only two, and not comfortably. Tessie opened the smaller door to reveal a set of stairs down into the gloom.

"Flashlight," she said, and the device was passed like a baton, from the rear of the pack to Rob to the cameraman to her; she flicked it on and pointed it down the stairs. Cobwebs lined the walls and fine soot covered the ramshackle wooden steps. Tessie tried the stability of the first step by putting half her weight on it, then all; the stairway bore her without so much as a creak. Tessie moved further into the maw of the basement.

"Be careful," said Rob, but his voice was distant, so far away.

Tessie descended, the flashlight aimed at each subsequent step. Down, down, down. The stairs seemed never-ending; how far down could the basement be? At some point, she no longer heard the cameraman following her. She turned to see where he had gone, but the view behind her mirrored the one ahead of her: stairs, rising instead of falling, though it became difficult to tell the difference. An infinite stairwell, no way in or out, the walls narrower than when she first entered.

Tessie decided to change direction and ascended, taking steps two at a time, leaning forward and gaining speed, until she'd climbed thrice as many as she'd descended and her thighs burned with exertion, but every time she raised her head to look forward, more stairs greeted her, stretching off into the darkness. Sweat dripped down her temples and the nape of her neck, and she gasped for breath, but made no progress.

Down it was, then.

She turned around to descend and her foot slipped on the silky layer of soot. She dropped the flashlight and pulled herself into the fetal position, a toppling ball, but the sharp corners of the wooden steps bruised her back and head and shins with each bounce. She tumbled and tumbled, the edges of the steps jabbing her, and the sharp pains took her breath away. She had no sense of how long she'd been falling or how much longer she would fall. The universe was the stairwell, her world the stairs. This was all there was, and all there would ever be.

And then she slammed into something. Her body throbbed and her ears rang. In the background, an irregular knock-clank-knock-knock, too sharp for footsteps, became louder with each burst of sound; when the chaotic beam of light appeared in the distance, she realized her flashlight had followed her. It came to a rest at her feet. She grabbed it, and pointed it forward to investigate what had broken her fall.

A door whose knots and whorls were arranged in an intimately familiar pattern, although she couldn't place where she'd seen it before. She rubbed it with the palm of her hand, and its texture reminded her powerfully of something—what was it?—surely she'd seen this door ten thousand times over.

She pushed it open, and—the raggedy twin beds filling nearly half the room, the faded posters on the walls, the mangy hand-me-down toys she loved and hated.

A step into the room, and the door melded into the wall behind her. She was trapped in this museum of her worst memories, this cell she'd never planned to revisit. It was smaller than she remembered—everything was smaller now—this cruelly cramped sanctum-turned-jail where she'd hidden so often but never completely escaped.

One bed was tidy and the other—hers—was a wreck. A layer of dust coated the neatly-made bed. Tessie dared not touch it, not now, not then. She wondered what her own life would have been like had she too escaped.

How had she spent so much time in this tiny space, with room enough for only one of her and her sister to get into bed at a time, no shelves, no windows, such a sparse shell of a room? A block of wood for a nightstand, holding a simple lamp. Nothing more. Well—something more. Something that made her life bearable. Something carefully hidden.

Would it be there? Tessie explored between the mattress and box spring of her bed, reaching by memory for where she'd hidden it. A single issue of *Discover* magazine. Her parents would have torn it to shreds if they'd found it. It had been displayed on the newsstand where her friends had stopped for candy on the way home from school every day, and she'd saved her change—money had been scarce and her parents had earned none, even appropriating her meager savings—to afford to buy the issue that read "50 Most Important Women in Science" in the top corner. Her friends had teased her for spending her money on a boring science magazine. She didn't care. They could have their candy bars and comic books; she wanted to read about math and physics and astronomy and archaeology.

Tessie pulled the magazine out, and it looked as she remembered it, worn and lovingly dog-eared. She'd memorized every last bit of it. She flipped through the pages, and the articles comforted her like old friends. She knew the next word of each piece before reading it, like singing along to a favorite song, and the photographs evoked memories of reading late at night, over and over, fearful of being caught in the act, but exhilarated at the stories of scientific achievement. It was a miracle her sister had never ratted her out. They'd stuck together, though. They had only each other, right up until the moment her sister abandoned her, disappearing into the night.

Tessie turned the issue over in her hands, inspecting the front and back covers. She'd spent hours staring at the rippled blue waters of the shoreline, the archaeological apparatus set up to perform an underwater dig, primed to uncover an ancient civilization. Memories flooded her mind: the joy of discovery, the ecstasy of hope, the yearning of wanting to be more. The dream of escape. That cover had inspired her to want to be an archaeologist. A true archaeologist, not someone digging for fake remnants of fake spirits.

"I'll show you fake. What's that you're reading?"

Tessie spun around to see her mother, restored to youth, a sneer on her face. "Leave me alone," Tessie said.

"Getting uppity, are we? Give me that." She thrust her hand out and waited for Tessie to surrender the magazine.

"No," said Tessie, holding the pages tight to her chest. She was cornered between the beds, her mother in front of her and a wall behind, no space to maneuver, and no place to escape.

Her mother patted her sister's bed, sending motes of dust swirling. "You know, you're the reason she left," she said. "She couldn't stand you. None of us can stand you. Always trying to be better than us."

"She left because of you and dad."

Her mother drew closer. Tessie shrank away from the phantasm. This was not her real mother.

"I'm as real as you are, dearie." Her mother lunged for the magazine and Tessie parried her grab, but she didn't see her mother's other hand as it swung full force and struck her in the head.

The blow dazed Tessie and her mother snatched the magazine. "Give it back!" said Tessie, her voice thin and childlike.

"Your father will deal with you," said her mother, and disappeared, magazine and all.

Tessie fell onto her bed. Her treasure—gone. She punched her pillow and threw it across the room. She tore her bed apart, strewing the bedclothes across the floor, and then started on her sister's, sending a cloud of dust into the air, so thick it might have been billowing smoke. The walls resisted her pounding and kicking and left her with bruised hands and aching feet.

Tessie wondered how long she'd have to wait for the phantasm of her father to show up.

"I'm finished here," she yelled to no one in particular.

The room shook.

"You have no power over me," she said.

"Says the girl with nowhere to go," boomed a voice, everywhere and nowhere at once, that might have originated from within her own head, had the foundations of the room not shuddered.

"Face me," said Tessie.

The room vibrated, and Tessie couldn't tell if the floor shook or if she did.

"Enough tricks," she said.

Tessie blinked, and her father towered before her, eyes shot red, a belt in his hands. Had she shrunk? She looked down at herself: she no longer wore her smart jacket and blouse and muddied jeans, but her most hated pair of pajamas, flannel and ratty and gifted to her in charity long ago. She was a little girl again, trapped in her 11-year old body.

"That's enough from you," he said, snapping the belt.

"You're not going to hit me," said Tessie. Her voice was pitched higher in her ears.

Her father squinted at her. "What are you talking about, girl?" He snapped the belt again. He reared back and Tessie crossed her arms to protect herself. Her mind raced. Was this a memory? Her father had been mean, and a deadbeat, and a bad husband to her mother, but never physically violent. That was her mother's area.

The belt came down across Tessie's arms, and she cried out as it stung the bruises from her tumble down the stairs. The situation was eerily familiar. Had she repressed memories of abuse? No—her father was much too much of a sad sack to strike her. Or had the memory of his latter days softened her image of him, days when he was too constantly drunk to stand, never mind physically discipline her?

"Pay attention when I'm talking to you, little girl," he growled, raising his arm again.

Tessie closed her eyes and concentrated on the image of the magazine cover. The feeling of hope. It wasn't too late to be an archaeologist. It would never be too late. She could start by using her rationality to escape this nightmare, whatever it was. The belt came down, but Tessie wouldn't allow the pain to define her.

She hadn't been chasing ghosts all these years, she'd been running from them. Pretending they didn't follow her, didn't infect every moment of her life. Using her cynicism as armor. She'd perfected the art of denial long before she'd become a professional skeptic. Maybe she was wrong, and Rob was right: she'd been blinded by her zeal to deny all she didn't understand. She admitted to herself something she'd known in her heart ever since the original envelope arrived with its unshakable chill: the supernatural was at work here.

But how did it work, exactly? Tessie pored over the evidence. Each time she'd been seized by a vision, she'd been back to normal shortly after, with no lingering physical effects. This entity was controlling her mind. As she stood there in her childhood bedroom, arms crossed, absorbing strokes from the belt, she pictured herself frozen on camera, Rob and the other crew members trying to prompt her. That was reality, not this.

If the entity used her own mind against her, she could fight back. This was her turf. She opened her eyes and straightened up, a grown woman again, eye-to-eye with her father. Her not-father. The man she knew was pathetic and verbally abusive, and the thing in front of her was a caricature, a perversion designed to enhance his most despicable attributes. He swung and she grabbed the belt as it came forward.

"You have no power here." She pulsed the words through gritted teeth, and rage and despondency, and hope and desire filled her.

Her not-father grunted and tried to wrestle the belt from her, but Tessie held strong. She swung her fist at the phantasm, this bricolage of her memory, cobbled from pieces of her subconscious, animated by something ancient and indescribable. Her punch connected with the side of its head. It yelled, and her mother appeared, and the waitress Meggie, and the cop, all of them screaming at her, but Tessie concentrated on her own burgeoning power. Her mind's eye exploded with images of ripples of the blue water, and more: the portraits of all the women who'd conquered so much to become the most important scientists of their generation. Her childhood memories of hope washed over her. It wasn't too late.

"You didn't deserve to attend any of those universities," said her non-mother. "Why would they want you? You have nothing to give to this world. You should know your place." Tessie ignored her. "I'm dying, and you're shitting around with this reality show." The phantasm's conviction was fading. "You'll never be anything."

Tessie's hope wrapped around her like a blanket, and she banished the specters with a flash of pale golden light. When the shimmer faded, the room had returned to its original state, with one difference: her mother lay in her sister's bed—her old, sick, dying mother, the woman she'd left behind to film this last ghost-hunting journey. She turned her jaundiced eyes to Tessie, and croaked, "You should be home, taking care of me."

Tessie said, "You don't need my help."

Her mother lay still and closed her eyes, as tears welled in Tessie's. The room became a blur. She turned to where she'd entered and the vague outline of a door had reappeared. She reached to open it, and a voice distant, so far away, said, "Be careful."

She blinked the tears out of her eyes and she stood in the boiler room, the cameraman behind her and the shabby door that had led to the infinite stairwell in front. She opened the door to find it a rough-in. It was a dead-end.

Chapter Nine

Tessie sat across from Rob in the airport cafe, where tired, delayed travelers shuffled about, looking for their next connection. A mild snow had overtaken the area.

She swirled the last bit of coffee in her styrofoam cup. The grounds peeked through the depression at the center of the whirlpool before sinking back down below the surface. It was the best cup of coffee she'd had in the last few days, hands down. And she needed it.

"How do you feel?" asked Rob, his eyes bloodshot.

"About the way you look," said Tessie. "Did they give you any information about X?"

"No," said Rob. "Nothing."

The police had descended on the production, warrants in hand, and demanded its closure. They pulled in the cast and crew for interrogation; an officer had disappeared the previous day. Rob and Tessie spent the night at the station, waiting to answer questions, then answering questions, then waiting for everyone else to answer questions. The police concluded the two of them were not persons of interest and let them go in time—barely—to make their flights.

Tessie had told the truth, nothing but the truth, but perhaps not the whole truth.

Rob sighed, looking more tired than Tessie had ever seen him. He stared at a point just over Tessie's left shoulder, tilted his head slightly, squinted, and then returned to the here and now.

"I'm sure he'll turn up," said Tessie, but she knew he wouldn't. Neither would the cop or the diner waitress. She wondered why they deserved to be victims of the house, and she did not.

"There's been a rash of disappearances over the last few days," said Rob.

"They told you that?" asked Tessie.

"I have my sources." Rob smiled weakly. "We shouldn't be surprised. This town is known for it. The house's thrall extends quite a ways, I suppose."

"You know," said Tessie, her voice cracking, "I don't believe in all that."

"Are you sure?"

Tessie stared at her coffee. A few brown specks floated lazily on the surface.

Rob continued. "You were pretty preoccupied during filming. What was going on?"

She shrugged. "What do you want me to say?"

"It doesn't matter, I guess," he replied. "Didn't manage to capture much of anything on film." He looked into her eyes. "Tell me you believe."

"Is that what you really want?" she asked.

"We're trending on social media," he said. "I'm expecting the best ratings we've ever had. We must've done something right."

Tessie knew what was coming next.

"Let's do another, Tessie. I've got a tip on this hotel room. The room number digits add to thirteen and..."

Tessie shook her head slowly, sadly. "No, Rob," she said. "I'm done."

Her phone buzzed in her pocket. She'd almost forgotten the police had returned it to her. She checked the screen: Natalie. "I have to take this."

Tessie moved to a quieter corner of the cafe, adjacent to the windows overlooking the runway. Planes lined up in a horseshoe formation, waiting for clearance to depart. The queue was moving, despite the flakes. The snow blanketed the trees in the far distance, haunting and beautiful.

"Everything okay?" she asked.

Static greeted her on the other end of the line. Tessie listened for hidden voices in the noise, but heard nothing.

"Natalie?"

A stifled sob.

"Natalie!"

"I," came a voice, finally. "I tried to call you yesterday, when it happened." An intake of breath, catching in Natalie's throat, and a cough. "Been trying to call you all night, but I couldn't get through. I'm sorry!"

"What's wrong?"

"She's gone."

Tessie had known already, somehow. She watched the procession of planes move forward, the puddle jumper at its head taking off. "My flight leaves soon," she said. "You'll be all right?"

"I should be. I didn't expect..." Natalie started again, this time with more composure. "I didn't expect to care so much."

"I'll be there in a few hours. As fast as I can."

"Promise?" said Natalie.

"Promise."

When Tessie returned to the table, Rob was texting away—no doubt planning his next adventure with his mysterious contacts. He looked up at her. "Everything okay?"

"It will be," said Tessie.

"You sure you won't come back for another go? Nothing I can say to change your mind?"

Tessie thought of Natalie dealing with their mother's death. Of how she'd needed Natalie's help, and how Natalie would now need hers. Of Anastasia, and the chance to be a cool aunt. Of grad schools, and how even being admitted as a publicity stunt would still give her the same access as any other student. And of everything else that could lie ahead of her, if only she took the opportunity.

"No," she said. "It's time to move on."

Acknowledgements

No book is written alone, even a short one like this! I'd like to thank my wife Ann Priestman for her love and support. Thanks to the South Shore Scribes for reading the first draft, two thousand words at a time. I had great beta readers: Shipra Agarwal, Nicole Dillie, Chris Johnson, Christine Lajewski, Jessica Lévai, and Heather Randolph. Special shoutout to Nicole, Christine, and Jessica for giving me feedback to make sure I did justice to Tessie's point of view as a woman; another special shoutout to Shipra for her sheer enthusiasm for the story, which helped inspire me to keep writing it! Thanks to Tasha Reynolds for proofreading. Typos are sneaky buggers, and any that remain are my fault alone. And finally, thanks to Ruth Anna Evans, for taking a chance on a debut novella, for pushing me to make edits that improved the cohesiveness of the story, for the wonderful cover, and for the rest of her great work as a publisher.

ABOUT THE AUTHOR

Christopher Degni writes about the magic and the horror that lurk just under the surface of everyday life. He has published numerous short stories in venues such as *99 Tiny Terrors*, *99 Fleeting Fantasies*, *Deadman Humour: Fears of Clown*, *Sherlock Holmes and the Occult Detectives*, and *Stupefying Stories*. He was part of the editorial team for the Stoker-nominated *MOTHER: Tales of Love and Terror* and the music-horror anthology *Playlist of the Damned*. He is a graduate of the Odyssey Writing Workshop, and currently lives south of Boston with his wife.

Author's Note

You made it to the end! If you want to help *Ghostshow Live!* succeed, please consider:

1. *Buying a copy.* Well, you're here, reading this, so you probably already have. Thank you! I appreciate it!

2. *Rating and reviewing on Amazon and/or Goodreads.* Reviews on these sites give books more visibility, which helps other readers find them.

3. *Telling all your friends, especially the ones who you think would love the book.* Indie authors don't have a lot of money for big marketing campaigns, so

we rely heavily on word of mouth. If you know someone you think would love this book, please tell them about it!

Thanks again for reading! I hope that you enjoyed the book, that it made you think, and, of course, that it scared you!

-Chris

9 798987 819548